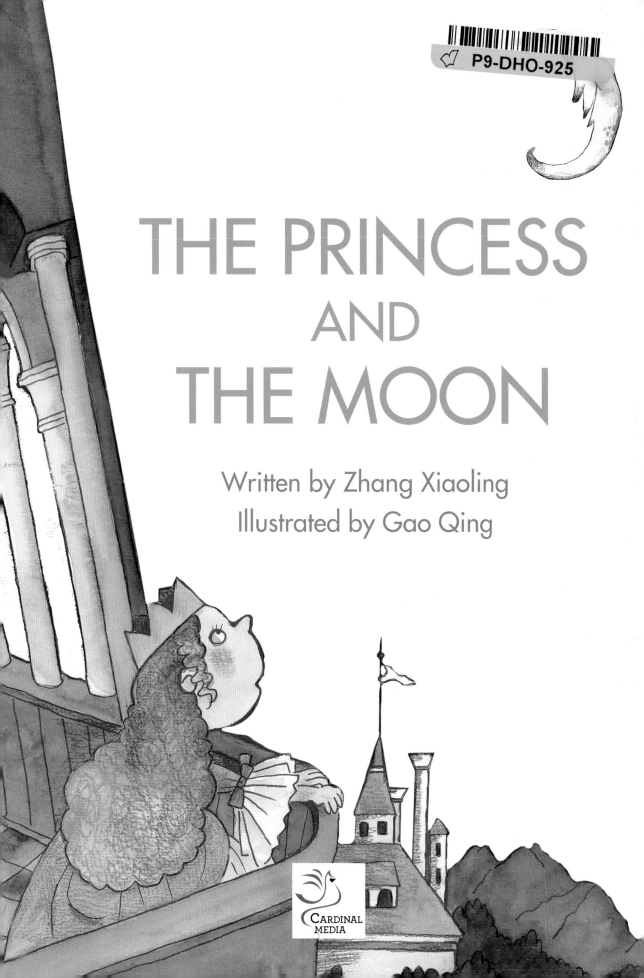

THE PRINCESS AND THE MOON

Written by Zhang Xiaoling

Illustrated by Gao Qing

CARDINAL MEDIA

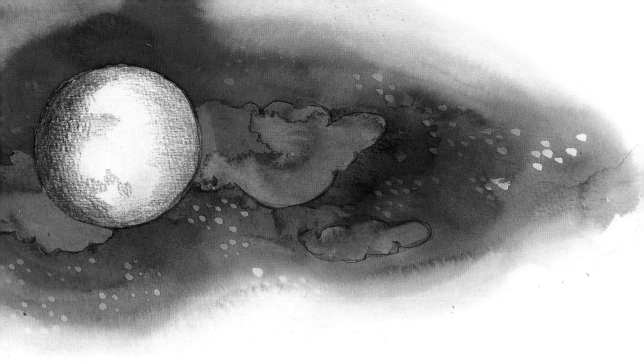

Once upon a time, there was a princess who lived in a kingdom. Every year on her birthday, the princess got to eat a special treat.

This year, when the king asked her what treat she'd like, she said, "I've already tried every good thing to eat in the world. I want something different. I wish to eat the MOON!"

The king wanted to grant her special wish.

But *how*?

He asked his royal court for ideas.

The Duke said, "Instead of letting her eat the moon, we could paint a picture of the moon for her."

The Duchess said, "We could bake her a cake in the shape of the moon."

The Earl said, "At night we could scoop out the moon's reflection in the castle moat and make moon soup."

However, the little princess was not satisfied.

The king posted a notice at the palace gates. It read:

Whoever can take the moon from the sky
for the princess to eat
will be rewarded with a whole town.

A boy took down the notice. He told the royal guards, "Let the king know that *I* will be the one to fulfill the princess's wish."

That evening, the boy was invited to the palace.

The full moon shone brightly in the sky.
The princess pointed at it and told the boy,
"Bring me the moon!"

The boy replied, "The moon is too big. It is not
possible to have the entire moon at one time,
but I could cut off a thin slice."

The princess was not impressed, but she decided
to give him a chance. "Very well," she said.
"Tomorrow bring me a slice of the moon."

The next evening, the boy returned to the palace. In his arms, he carried something long and curved.

"What is *that*?" demanded the princess.

"It's the moon," replied the boy.

The princess took a closer look. "This is nothing but a piece of bread!" she said.

The boy said, "That's not true. Look at the sky."

The princess looked up and saw that the moon was missing a small slice. The missing part of the moon was *exactly the same shape as the bread*.

The boy smiled and said, "You wanted to eat the moon, Princess? Well, now you can."

The princess was stubborn. "I will not eat it until you bring me the whole moon," she said.

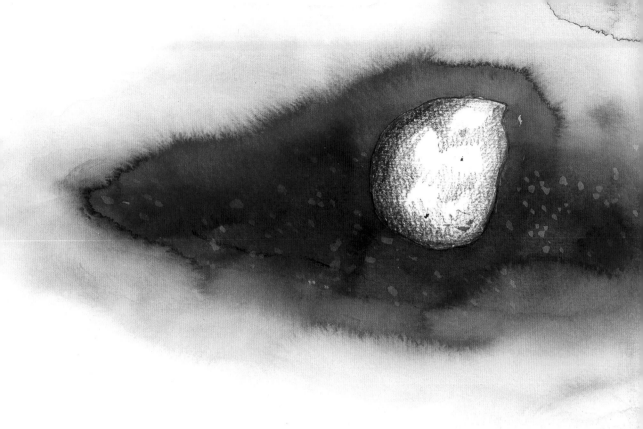

The following evening, the boy returned to the palace with another slice of the moon.

He told the princess to check the night sky. Sure enough, the moon was missing another slice.

The boy put both pieces of the moon together in a basket for the princess.

The next night the boy brought another slice to the princess. The moon in the sky grew smaller, while the moon in her basket became bigger.

After a few nights, the princess began
to look forward to the boy's visits.
They'd watch the night sky together.

"The moon looks so beautiful," the princess
said one night.

"You didn't notice the moon before?"
the boy asked.

The princess shook her head. "I didn't have
anyone to watch it with me," she said.

By the eighth night, both the moon in the sky
and the moon in the basket were exactly half
of a circle. The princess was very happy.

The moon in the basket kept growing while the moon in the sky got smaller. One evening, while the princess and the boy were watching the moon together, she asked, "If you keep cutting slices of the moon for me, will the moon in the night sky disappear?"

The boy said, "You'll just have to find out."

After two weeks passed, the boy delivered the last piece of the moon. Now the princess had the whole moon in her basket!

It was everything she'd wished for, but now something was not right. She rushed onto the balcony. The night sky was pitch black, with no moon in sight.

The princess burst into tears and ran to the king.

"I don't want the moon anymore!" she cried.

"Why not?" asked the king.

"The moon belongs in the night sky!" she said.

The king asked the boy to put the moon back into the sky. He promised the boy that he'd still receive the reward.

The boy agreed.

He held up one piece of the moon from the basket. Then he asked the princess to invite some poor, hungry children to join them and eat it.

"The only way to return the moon to the night sky is to eat it," he explained.

So the Princess invited some children to the palace. That evening, they all ate the moon joyfully.

After they finished eating, a new moon appeared in the night sky.

The princess invited the children to return each night.

Piece by piece, they ate the moon from the basket.

Night by night, the moon in the sky grew larger.

After eating, they talked, played games, and watched the moon together.

The princess was very happy.

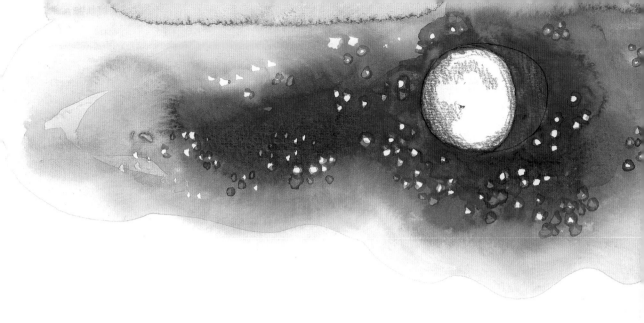

At last they finished eating the moon.
The basket was empty, and a full moon
appeared in the night sky.

As promised, the king rewarded the boy
with a town of his very own.

The princess began to cry.

"Now that the children and I have finished eating the moon, they won't come here any longer. I thought I had everything I could want in this world. I have even eaten the moon. But having all those things doesn't mean anything if I don't have anyone to share them with."

That evening, the princess sat alone
in the courtyard, watching the moon.
Suddenly she noticed that it was
missing a small piece.

The princess smiled. She knew who had done it.
She asked the king for permission to visit the
boy's town.

Sure enough, the boy had taken a slice of the moon and was sharing it with the hungry children in his town. He had prepared a whole feast for them.

The children were delighted to see the princess. "Come and join us!" they said.

The princess was so happy. She decided that she would come to the boy's town each day to play with the children, and together they would eat the moon.

A spoiled princess wants the moon for herself—to eat! When a clever boy finds a way to bring her the moon, what she really learns is the joy of sharing with others.

Cardinal Media, LLC.
8501 West Higgins Road, Suite 790
Chicago, Illinois 60631
www.cardinalmediakids.com

ISBN 978-1-64074-008-2

9 781640 740082

90000

Printed in China